McBroom the Rainmaker

Library of Congress Cataloging-in-Publication Data

Fleischman, Sid, 1920-
  McBroom the rainmaker / by Sid Fleischman ; illustrated by Amy Wummer.
    p. cm. — (The adventures of McBroom)
  Summary : When a great drought on the prairie causes cows to give powdered milk and
mosquitoes to grow almost as large as small cowsheds, McBroom comes up with a novel
idea for producing rain.
  [1. Rain and rainfall—Fiction. 2. Droughts—Fiction. 3. Farm life—Fiction. 4. Tall tales.
5. Humorous stories.] I. Wummer, Amy, ill. II. Title. III. Series: Fleischman, Sid, 1920-
Adventures of McBroom.   98-56264
PZ7.F5992Macr   1999   CIP
[Fic]—dc21   AC

ISBN 0-8431-7496-X   B C D E F G H I J

McBroom the Rainmaker

By **Sid Fleischman**

Illustrated by **Amy Wummer**

PSS!
PRICE STERN SLOAN

1

I dislike telling you this, but some folks have no regard for the truth. A stranger claims he was riding a mule past our wonderful one-acre farm and was attacked by woodpeckers.

Well, there's no truth to that. No, indeed! Those weren't woodpeckers. They were common prairie mosquitoes.

Small ones.

Why, skeeters grow so large out here that everybody uses chicken wire for mosquito netting. But I'm not going to say an unkind word about those zing-zanging, hot-tempered, needle-nosed creatures. They rescued our farm from ruin. That was during the Big Drought we had last year.

Dry? Merciful powers! Our young'uns found some polliwogs and had to teach them to swim. It hadn't rained in so long those tadpoles had never seen water.

That's the sworn truth—certain as my name's Josh McBroom. Why, I'd as soon grab a skunk by the tail as tell a falsehood.

Now, I'd best creep up on the Big
Drought the way it crept up on us. I
remember we did our spring plowing as
usual, and the skeeters hatched out as
usual. The bloodsucking rapscallions
could be mighty pesky, but we'd learned
to distract them. The thirsty critters
would drink up *anything* red.

"Will*jill*hester*chester*peter*polly*tim*tom*-mary*larry*andlittle*clarinda*!" I called out. "I hear the whine of gallinippers. Better put in a patch of beets."

Once the beets were up, the skeeters stuck in their long beaks like straws. Didn't they feast, though! They drained out the red juice, the beets turned white, and we harvested them as turnips.

The first sign of a dry spell coming was when our clocks began running slow. We grew our own clocks on the farm.

Vegetable clocks.

Now, I'll admit that may be hard to believe, but not if you understand the remarkable nature of our topsoil. Rich? Glory be! Anything would grow in it—lickety-bang. Three or four crops a day until the confounded Big Dry came along.

Of course, we didn't grow clocks with gears and springs and a name on the dial. Came close once, though. I dropped my dollar pocket watch one day, and before I could find it, the thing had put down roots and grown into a three-dollar alarm clock. But it never kept accurate time after that.

It was our young'uns who discovered they could tell time by vegetable. They planted a cucumber seed, and once the vine leaped out of the ground it traveled along steady as a clock.

"An inch a second," Will said. "Kind of like a second hand."

"Blossoms come out on the minute," Jill said. "Kind of like a minute hand."

They tried other vegetable timepieces, but pole beans had a way of running a mite fast and squash a mite slow.

As I say, those homegrown clocks began running down. I remember my dear wife Melissa was boiling three-and-a-half-minute eggs for breakfast. Little Clarinda planted a cucumber seed, and before it grew three blossoms and thirty inches those eggs were hardboiled.

"Mercy!" I declared. "Topsoil must be drying out."

But I wasn't worried. Rain would turn up.

What turned up was our neighbor, Heck Jones. Rusty nails stuck out of his bulging pockets. He was a tall, scrawny man with eyes shifty as minnows.

"*Hee-haw!*" he laughed. "Drought's a-comin'. You won't be able to grow weeds. Better buy some of my rain nails."

"Rain nails?" I said.

"Magnetized 'em myself." He grinned. "Secret formula, neighbor. Pound 'em in the ground and they'll draw rain clouds like flies to a garbage heap."

"Fiddle-faddle," I declared. "Flap-doodle, sir!"

"Why, only five dollars apiece. I'm merely trying to be of service, neighbor. Other farmers'll buy my rain nails—*hee-haw!*" And off he went, cackling through his nose.

Wasn't he an infernal scoundrel! I thought. Setting out to swindle his neighbors into buying rusty old nails at five dollars each!

Well, the days turned drier and drier.
No doubt about it—our wonderful topsoil
was losing some of its get-up-and-go.
Why, it took almost a whole day to raise a
crop of corn. The young'uns had planted
a plum tree, but all it would grow was
prunes. Dogs would fight over a dry
bone—for the moisture in it.

"Will*jill*hester*chester*peter*polly*tim*tom*mary*larry*andlittle*clarinda*!" I called. "Keep your eyes peeled for rain."

They took turns in the tree house scanning the skies, and one night Chester said, "Pa, what if it doesn't rain by Fourth of July? How'll we shoot off firecrackers?"

"Be patient, my lambs," I said. We used to grow our own firecrackers, too. Don't let me forget to tell you about it. "Why, it's a long spell to Fourth of July."

My, wasn't the next morning a
scorcher! The sun came out so hot that
our hens laid fried eggs. But no, that
wasn't the Big Dry. The young'uns
planted watermelons to cool off and
beets to keep the mosquitoes away.

"Look!" Polly exclaimed, pointing to
the watermelons. "Pa, they're rising off
the ground!"

Rising? They began to float in the air
like balloons! We could hardly believe our
eyes. And gracious me! When we cut
those melons open, it turned out they
were full of hot air.

"*Hee-haw!*" Heck Jones laughed. There he stood jingling the rusty nails in his pocket. "Better buy some rain nails. Only ten dollars apiece."

I shot him a scowl. "You've doubled the price, sir."

"True, neighbor. And the weather's double as dry. Big Drought's a-comin'— it's almost here. How many ten-dollar rain nails do you want?"

"Flim-flam!" I answered stoutly. "None, sir!"

And off he went, cackling through his
nose. Drought wasn't a worry to him.
Heck Jones was such a shiftless farmer
that he could carry a whole year's harvest
in a tin cup. Now he was making himself
rich peddling flim-flam, flapdoodle,
fiddle-faddle rain attractors. Farmers all
over the county were hammering those
useless, rusty old nails into the ground.
They were getting desperate.

Well, I was getting a mite worried myself. Our beets were growing smaller and smaller, and the skeeters were growing larger and larger. Many a time, before dawn, a rapping at the windows would wake us out of a sound sleep. It was those confounded, needle-nosed gallinippers pecking away, demanding breakfast.

Then it came—the Big Dry.

Mercy! Our cow began giving powdered milk. We pumped away on our water pump, but all it brought up was steam. The oldest boys went fishing and caught six dried catfish.

"Not a rain cloud in sight, Pa," Mary called from the tree house.

"Watch out for gallinippers!" Larry shouted, as a mosquito made a dive at him. The earth was so parched we couldn't raise a crop of beets, and the varmints were getting downright ornery.

Then, as I stood there I felt my shoes getting tighter and tighter. I looked down. They must have shrunk two sizes!

"Thunderation!" I exclaimed. "Our topsoil's so dry it's gone in reverse. It's *shrinking* things."

Didn't I stay awake most of the night!
Our wonderful one-acre farm might
shrink to a square foot. And all night
long the skeeters rattled the windows
and hammered at the door. Big? The
smallest ones must have weighed three
pounds. In the moonlight I saw them
chase a yellow-billed cuckoo.

Didn't that make me sit up in a hurry!
An idea struck me. Glory be! I'd break
that drought.

First thing in the morning I took Will
and Chester to town with me and rented
three wagons and a birdcage. We drove
straight home, and I called everyone
together.

"Shovels, my lambs! Heap these
wagons full of topsoil!"

The mosquitoes were rising in swarms,
growing more temperish by the hour.

I heard a cackling sound and there stood Heck Jones. "*Hee-haw*, neighbor. Clearing out? Giving up? Why, I've got three nails left. Last chance."

"Sir," I said. "Your rusty old nails are a bamboozle and a hornswoggle. I intend to do a bit of rainmaking and break this drought!"

"*Hee-haw!*" he laughed, and ambled off.

Before long we were ready to go. It might be a longish trip, so we loaded up with picnic hampers, rolls of chicken wire, and our raincoats.

"Where are we going, Pa?" Jill called from one of the wagons.

"Hunting, my lambs. We're going to track down a rain cloud and wet down this topsoil."

"But how, Pa?" asked Tim.

I lifted the birdcage from under the wagon seat. "Presto," I said, and whipped off the cover. "Look at that lost-looking, scared-looking, long-tailed creature. Found it hiding from the skeeters under a milk pail this morning. It's a genuine rain crow, my lambs."

"A rain crow?" Mary said. "It doesn't look like a crow at all."

"Correct and exactly," I said, smiling. "It looks like a yellow-billed cuckoo, and that's what it is. But don't folks call 'em rain crows? Why, that bird can smell a downpour coming sixty miles away. Rattles its throat and begins to squawk. All we got to do is follow that squawk."

But you never heard such a quiet bird!
We traveled miles and miles across the
prairie, this way and the other, and not a
rattle out of that rain crow.

The Big Dry had done its mischief
everywhere. We didn't see a dog without
his tongue dragging, and it took two of
them to bark at us once.

A farmer told us he hadn't been able to
grow anything all year but baked potatoes!

We came to a field of sorghum cane, and our wagon wheels almost got stuck fast. I thought at first we had run over chewing gum. But no—that sweet cane had melted down to molasses and was dripping across the road.

Day after day we hauled our three loads of topsoil across the prairie, but that rain crow didn't so much as clear its throat.

The young'uns were getting impatient. "Speak up, rain crow," Chester muttered desperately.

"Rattle," Hester pleaded.

"Squawk," said Peter.

"Please," said Mary. "Just a peep would help."

Not a cloud appeared in the sky. I'll confess I was getting a mite discouraged. And the Fourth of July not another two weeks off!

We curled up under chicken wire that night, as usual, and the big skeeters kept banging into it so you could hardly sleep. Rattled like a hailstorm. And suddenly, at daybreak, I rose up laughing.

"Hear that?"

The young'uns crowded around the rain crow. We hadn't been able to hear its voice rattle for the mosquitoes.

Now it turned in its cage, gazed off to the northwest, opened its yellow beak, and let out a real, ear-busting rain cry. "K-*kawk!* K-*kawk!* K-*kawk!*"

"Put on your raincoats, my lambs!" I said, and we rushed to the wagons.

"K-*kawk!* K-*kawk!* K-*kawk!*"

Didn't we raise dust! That bird faced northwest like a dog on point. There was a rain cloud out there, and before long Jill gave a shout.

"I see it!"

And the others chimed in one after the other. "Me, too!"

"K-*kawk!* K-*kawk!* K-*kawk!*"

We headed directly for that lone cloud, the young'uns yelling, the horses snorting, and the bird squawking.

Glory be! The first raindrops spattered as large as quarters. And my, didn't the young'uns frolic in that cloudburst! They lifted their faces and opened their mouths and drank right out of the sky. They splashed about and felt mud between their toes for the first time in ages. We all forgot to put on our raincoats and got wet as fish.

Our dried-up topsoil soaked up
raindrops like a sponge. It was a joy
to behold! But if we stayed longer we'd
get stuck in the mud.

"Back in the wagons!" I shouted.
"Home, my lambs, and not a moment
to lose."

Well, home was right where we left it, and so was Heck Jones. He was fixing to give his house a fresh coat of paint—I reckoned with the money he'd got selling rusty nails. He'd even bought himself a skeeter-proof suit of armor and was clanking around in it.

He lifted the steel visor. "Howdy, neighbor. Come back to put your farm up for sale? I'll make you a generous offer. A nickel an acre."

"Preposterous, sir!" I replied, my temper rising.

"Why, farmers all over the county are ready to sell out if this drought doesn't break in twenty-four hours. Five cents an acre—that's my top price, neighbor."

"Our farm is not for sale," I declared. "And the drought is about over. I'm going to make rain."

"*Hee-haw*," he cackled. "The Big Drought's only half of it. You don't see any skeeters, do you? But they'll be back, and you'll wish you had a suit of armor, same as me. They chased the blacksmith out of his shop. Yup, and they're busy sharpening their noses on his grindstone. Sell, neighbor, and run for your lives."

"Never, sir," I answered.

But I did rush my dear wife Melissa and the young'uns into the house. Then I got a pinch of onion seeds and went from wagon to wagon, sowing a few seeds in each load of moist earth. I didn't want to crowd those onions.

Now, that rich topsoil of ours had been idle a long time—it was rarin' to go. Before I could run back to the house the greens were up. By the time I could get down my shotgun the tops had grown four or five feet tall—onions are terribly slow growers. Before I could load my shotgun the bulbs were finally busting up through the soil.

We stood at the windows watching. Those onion roots were having a great feast. The wagons heaved and creaked as the onions swelled and lifted themselves—they were already the size of pumpkins. But that wasn't near big enough. Soon they were larger'n washtubs and began to shoulder the smaller ones off the wagons.

47

Suddenly we heard a distant roaring in the air. Those zing-zanging, hot-tempered, bloodsucking prairie mosquitoes were returning from town with their stingers freshly sharpened. The Big Dry hadn't done their dispositions any good—their tempers were at a boil.

"You going to shoot them down, Pa?" Will asked.

"Too many for that," I answered.

"How big do those onions have to grow?" Chester asked.

"How big are they now?"

"A little smaller'n a cow shed."

"That's big enough." I nodded, lifting the window just enough to poke the shotgun through.

Well, the gallinippers spied the onions—I had planted blood-red onions, you know—and came swarming over our farm. I let go at the bulbs with a double charge of buckshot and slammed the window.

"Handkerchiefs, everyone!" I called out. The odor of fresh-cut onion shot through the air, under the door, and through the cracks. Cry? In no time our handkerchiefs were wet as dishrags.

Well! You never saw such surprised gallinippers. They zing-zanged every which way, most of them backward. And weep? Their eyes began to flow like sprinkling cans. Onion tears! The roof began to leak. Mud puddles formed everywhere. Before long the downpour was equal to any cloudburst I ever saw.

6

The skeeters kept their distance after
that. But they'd been mighty helpful.

With our farm freshly watered we grew
tons of great onions—three or four crops
a day. Gave them away to farmers all over
the county. We broke the Big Drought,
and that's how I came to be known as
McBroom the Rainmaker.

We didn't hear a *hee* or a *haw* out of
Heck Jones. Inside his clanking suit of
armor he grumbled and growled and
finished painting his house. And that
was a mistake, for the gallinippers hadn't
left the county. They had just flocked
off somewhere for a breath of fresh air.

Well, they flocked back. I was standing
with my shoes in the earth. My feet had
been a torment ever since our dry topsoil
had shrunk the leather.

"Little Clarinda," I said. "Kindly plant
a vegetable clock. I reckon it'll take one
minute exactly to grow these shoes two
sizes larger."

She planted a cucumber seed—and
that's when the gallinippers returned.
Flocks and flocks of them and, my, didn't
they look hungry! You could see their
ribs standing out. They headed for Heck
Jones's house as if he'd rung the dinner
bell. That ornery, wily neighbor of ours
had painted his house a fool-headed red.

Well! The huge skeeters dropped like hawks. They speared the wood siding with their long, grindstone-sharpened stingers. Must have gone clear through, for we could see Heck Jones in the windows, hammering over the tips.

Oh, he was chuckling and cackling. The gallinippers flapped their wings like caught roosters. Thousands of them! The next thing I knew, all those flapping wings lifted the house a few inches. Then a foot. I was surprised to see the floor remain behind—I reckoned Heck Jones had pulled the nails to sell. Then those prairie mosquitoes gave a mighty heave— and flew off. With the house.

Little Clarinda and I were so dumb-
founded we'd forgot about the cucumber
clock! It had grown thirty-seven blossoms.
I tripped over my own feet, and no
wonder! My shoes had grown more'n a
yard long.

"K-*kawk!* K-*kawk!* K-*kawk!*"

Glory be! Rain—and it wasn't long in coming. I almost felt sorry for Heck Jones the next day. He could be seen walking his floor without a roof over his head in the downpour.

The young'uns had a splendid Fourth of July. Grew all the fireworks they wanted. They'd dash about with beanshooters—shooting radish seeds into the ground. You know how fast radishes come up. In our rich topsoil they grew quicker'n the eye. The seeds hardly touched the ground before they took root and swelled up and exploded. They'd go off like strings of firecrackers.

And, mercy, what a racket! At nightfall a scared cat ran up a tree, and I went up a ladder to get it down. Reached in the branches and caught it by the tail.

I'd be lying if I didn't admit the truth. It was a skunk.